Febe & THE ZOYLAND FAIRIES

Published by Fizazzle
Written by Tanya Quinn
Illustrated by Donna Brazier

ISBN: 978-981-07-242-8

'Strange Creatures in the Woods'

Written by Tanya Quinn
Illustrated by Donna Brazier

It is a beautiful spring morning in Zoyland, the sun is shining and the birds have all come out to play. Febe rises early with excitement, because today she has planned an adventure...

Last night Febe's best friend Petal gave her news of a mysterious creature in the woods. Febe has decided to go and search for it. Petal said the creature is as big as a house, it is bright red and yellow and has eyes that burn orange as if on fire.

The thought of seeing this creature and discovering what it could be is so exciting that Febe just can't wait to go on her quest!

She gathers up a few things; an apple in case she gets hungry and her wand in case of an emergency.
With everything packed she sets off on her adventure.

She wants to go to a spot where the creature has been seen. She flies for miles and miles, over rocks and trees, crossing many rivers and fields.

Eventually Febe arrives at the spot. She knows the place
well as she has been there many times before. The huge
boulder which marks the spot towers above the undergrowth.
But.... there is no sign of the mysterious creature.

As she waits she sings songs with the birds and marvels at the ants that march by. Hours pass, but still there is no sign of the strange creature. It will soon be dark and Febe is a long way from home.

As night closes in, back in Zoyland
Febe's best friend Petal is worried.
She has noticed that Febe has not
returned and decides to go and search for her.

Meanwhile Febe is still determined to see the creature and has decided to stay the night. She cannot sleep and stares into the darkness. Then a faint flicker of light appears in the sky. What a beautiful bright star Febe thinks.

As the light gets closer it doubles in size. Bigger and bigger it grows. All of a sudden Febe realises it is the strange creature that she has been waiting for!

It is a Firebird, it's beauty is magnificent.
Febe is captivated, she cannot take her eyes away.
As she watches, the firebird glides to the ground
and its flames gradually burn out.

The feathers start to float off the bird and fill the sky. 'How strange,' Febe thinks, as she watches in disbelief. Then as if by magic, the feathers that are hitting the boulder transform into...

...little men ???

Febe cannot believe what she is seeing.
What are the men doing?

How did the Firebird shed it's feathers and disappear to leave behind hundreds of little men? Febe is curious and decides she has to get closer.

She quietly creeps closer to the boulder trying not to
make a sound. But then "Crack", Febe stepped on a twig,
and all the little men turn. They look at her angrily.
"Oops, sorry" says Febe. "I was only trying to..."

The little men are not happy and swarm around Febe..
Luckily Petal has just arrived at the boulder. She see's
what is happening and senses that Febe is in trouble.

Petal runs very fast back to Zoyland. "Come quickly," she screams as she whizzes through the town, banging on every hut and shelter that she can find, "Febe is in trouble and she needs our help!"

What's happened?" the Zoyland folk ask.
"Hundreds of little men have surrounded Febe",
says Petal "and they look angry. We must
rescue her. There's no time to lose!"

Overhead Elder Owl is listening. Elder Owl is wise and he knows what the little men are. "The Little men are Zorrocks", Elder Owl explains. "You must hurry, Febe is in great danger! You must divert the Zorrock's attention as their eyes can turn you into stone!" Petal is now very worried.

Elder Owl continues,"Take this mirror. If the Zorrocks look in the mirror they themselves will be turned to stone and their hold on Febe will be broken." All the Zoyland fairies and creatures race into the woods to rescue Febe.

When they arrive they are horrified. It is too late! Febe has already been turned to stone. The Zorrocks are celebrating, creating the most horrible screeching noise. Petal races towards Febe with the mirror held high sheilding their eyes. She hopes that Elder Owl's plan will work.

Soon the forest goes quiet again, Petal cautiously lowers the mirror. To her relief the plan has worked. All of the Zorrocks have seen themselves in the mirror and have turned themselves to stone.

Petal turns to see her friend stood firm and cries, "I'm so sorry Febe I tried, I was as quick as I could be. I'm so sorry." Tears roll down Petal's cheeks and fall on Febe's hands.

With that there is a loud gasp and the spell is broken. Febe is back! The Zoyland fairies are so relieved and happy. They quickly usher her back home, where they will be safe.

They celebrate their escape from the Zorrocks and Febe's return by dancing until morning.

- The End -

'Party with Febe and Friends'

Febe and the Zoyland Fairies are now available for childrens parties and events in Singapore.
For party bookings and event services contact -
www.fizazzle.com
www.fairyfebe.com

More Febe and the Zoyland Fairies books coming soon, keep an eye out for Febe's next adventure.
"When the Lights went Out"